# A MESSAGE
## FROM
# ALLAN

## LYNETTE ALLI
### Illustrations by Kersly Miñoza

To order additional copies of this book, contact:
Xlibris LLC
1-888-795-4274
www.Xlibris.com
Orders@Xlibris.com

To the children of the world, be happy. You are beautiful.

For all the children of the world

Do not be afraid and

tell an adult if you are being bullied

Sincere thanks to my husband Akbar, daughter, Nezie and son in law Raymond, for your help and support.

My name is Allan, but they called me Alien. They kicked me, pushed me, and even spat on me. All because I came from another school.

This all started when my dad got a new job and we moved to another city. My sister and I were transferred to Paradise Elementary School in the middle of the school year.

My first day at the new school, I was very excited because I would make new friends. My teacher, Ms. Brown, welcomed me to her class.

She said, "Good morning, boys and girls, we have a new student who would be joining our class today."

The children said, "Good morning, Ms. Brown."

The teacher showed me my seat. I smiled and said "Hi" to the boy sitting next to me.

During the first recess, I played with most of the children, who were very nice to me. However, I noticed three boys from my class staring at me. Their names were Sam, Jack, and Tom. I wondered why they chose not to play with us.

Later that day at lunch, the teacher marked our math and gave it back in the afternoon session. Ms. Brown also said to the class, "Boys and girls, Allan, our new student, had the highest mark in math, and I am very impressed with his work. I am expecting everyone to do as well as him." I was given a certificate with a happy face with the word *excellent.*

The three boys, who did not play with us at first recess, did not like the praise I got from our teacher. This started the bullying, which began from the last recess, the first day. During this recess, the three boys, surrounded me. Sam, the bigger one, said, "You do not belong here. Go back to your old school, Alien. " They then shoved and kicked me, chanting, "Alien, Alien, teacher's pet."

During my first week, I tried to tell them several times, my name is Allan, but they continued to call me Alien. On Friday, it was cookie day at the new school, and the three boys took my cookie. This, with the other abuse, continued for over a month.

I was sad, hurt, and scared. I have heard and read about children who were being bullied, but now I knew their pain and fear. I suffered the same way.

One day I asked my sister Ann, "Do you like your new school?"

Ann replied, "Yes! I loved my new school and my new friends. Why did you ask?"

I replied, "Just checking."

I pretended to be sick one day, and my parents called to inform the school. This worked the first time, so I faked my illness several times not to go to school. My parents became worried about my sudden illness. They took me to my doctor for a checkup, and he said everything looked normal. While my parents were happy with the results, they were still concerned about me.

My grades began to drop, and I thought the boys would stop bullying me, but they continued. My teacher was worried about the sudden drop in my grades, and she contacted my parents, who agreed to meet with her.

The meeting was with my parents, my teacher, and me. During the meeting, I felt sick. I broke down and explained everything about the bullying. I told them the names of the boys, and my teacher was surprised since she observed all the children were very nice to me during her lessons. She then found out this bullying took place during recess. My parents were upset with me for not telling them. I told them that I was afraid the boys would hurt me if I did not follow their rules.

The same day, the teacher reported the case of bullying to the principal, Mr. Gray, who took this matter very seriously. The boys were called to the principal's office. Even though they apologised to me, they were suspended for a week. The three boys and I were told by Mr. Gray that counselling sessions would be arranged for us, which we took later.

For all the children of the world

Do not be afraid and

tell an adult if you are being bullied

I sometimes had nightmares with the experiences I had with the other boys, but with the support from my parents and teacher, I was able, after some time, to overcome my fear.

My message to all children is this: Tell an adult the first time you are being bullied. Do not be afraid.

CPSIA information can be obtained
at www.ICGtesting.com
Printed in the USA
LVIC06n2146010415
432723LV00003B/4